JALEN'S BIG CITY LIFE

ONSTAGE JITTERS

T0372101

by **Dorothy H Price** illustrated by **Shiane Salabie**

raintree
a Capstone company — publishers for children

Raintree is an imprint of Capstone Global Library Limited,
a company incorporated in England and Wales having its
registered office at 264 Banbury Road, Oxford, OX2 7DY –
Registered company number: 6695582

Edited by Alison Deering
Designed by Jaime Willems
Production by Whitney Schaefer

Design element: Shutterstock: Alexzel, Betelejze,
cuppuccino, wormig

978 1 3982 5322 3

British Library Cataloguing in Publication Data
A full catalogue record for this book is available from the
British Library.

Printed and bound in India.

CONTENTS

MEET JC

Hi! My name is Jalen Corey Pierce, but everyone calls me JC. I am seven years old.

I live with Mum, Dad and my baby sister, Maya. Nana and Pop-Pop live in our block of flats too. So do my two best friends, Amir and Vicky.

My family and I used to live in a small town. Now I live in a big city with tall buildings and lots of people. Come along with me on all my new adventures!

Chapter 1

AUDITIONS

JC and his friends loved

going to the community centre.

One Saturday morning, they

saw something exciting. The

community centre was putting

on a play!

"I've always wanted to be in a play," Vicky said.

"Me too!" Amir agreed.

JC had been to the theatre with his family to see a play. But he'd never been in one. Being onstage sounded fun, especially with his friends.

"Let's do it together!" JC said.

Lots of kids came to the audition. Mrs Belfield, the community centre leader, was there too. She would be the director.

"We are going to be performing *The Pirate's Gold*," she told them. "There are lots of different roles. Each one is important. Relax and have fun."

Everyone recited the same lines. Amir went first, then Vicky.

Soon it was JC's turn to read.

He felt nervous.

What if I don't get a role? he

thought. But he tried his best.

"Who will find the gold?"

he said. "Argh! It'll be me!"

At the end, Mrs Belfield smiled at everyone.

"Well done!" she said. "I'll post the cast list here next Saturday. Good luck!"

Chapter 2

A BIG ROLE

THE PIRATE'S GOLD
Cast List

J.C. ....Pirate

Amir...............................Pirate's Assistant

Ashley.................................Navigator

Vicky..........................Petey the Parakeet

Travis.................................Cabin Boy

Jordan....................Pirate Crew Member #1

James.....................Pirate Crew Member #2

Jennifer...................Pirate Crew Member #3

Brooke..............................Map Merchant

JC and his friends went back
to the community centre the next
weekend. A list of names had
been pinned to the notice board.

Vicky pointed. "That's my
name! I'm Petey the Parakeet."

"And mine!" Amir exclaimed. "I'm the pirate's assistant."

JC looked at the list. "I'm in it too!" he cheered. "I'm a pirate!"

Mrs Belfield gave everyone a script. Vicky and Amir had four lines. JC had six lines.

"We'll meet every Saturday to rehearse," Mrs Belfield told the group. "The play is in one month. See you next week."

JC couldn't wait to tell his family about his big role.

"Congratulations!" said Mum.

"That is a big role," Dad said.

"You've got a lot of lines."

JC felt nervous again. *I hope I can remember all of them.*

Chapter 3

PRACTICE MAKES PERFECT

JC woke up with a plan.

He needed to practise. And he

only went to the community

centre on Saturdays. That

wasn't enough.

"Will you help me with my lines?" JC asked his parents. "I don't want to forget them onstage."

"Of course," Mum said.

"Start with one line at a time," Dad added. "Practice makes perfect."

Pirate's Assistant: Look here! There's something behind this rock.

Pirate runs to the rock and f the treasure.

ng last, I, Captair nally found th

d thro

Amir and Vicky came over later that day.

"I'm going to practise my lines for the play," JC told his friends.

"I need help with mine too," Vicky said.

"We can practise together," Amir suggested.

JC smiled. "Great idea!"

For the next three weeks, JC worked hard. He practised being a pirate with Mum and Dad.

He memorised lines with Vicky and Amir. And on Saturdays, everyone rehearsed their lines at the community centre.

By the end of the month, JC and his friends were ready!

Chapter 4

SHOWTIME!

It was finally showtime!

JC and his friends took their

places onstage. The curtain went

up. The lights were very bright.

Vicky and Amir said their lines

first. Then it was JC's turn.

The first five lines went well.

But then JC's nerves took over.

He forgot his last line.

A few seconds passed.

"Take a deep breath," Vicky

said quietly.

"You can do it," Amir

whispered.

JC remembered practising with his friends. He remembered being a pirate with Mum and Dad. He remembered rehearsing at the community centre.

Finally, JC remembered his line.

"All the gold and treasure belongs to me forever!" he exclaimed.

At the end of the play, the

entire cast took a bow.

"I knew you could do it,"

Mum said.

"That was a great play!"

added Dad.

JC smiled at his friends and said, "Arrr-en't you glad we did it together?"

GLOSSARY

audition trial performance for an actor or musician

cast actors performing in a show

director person who is in charge of a show

memorise learn something by heart so you can remember it without looking it up

nervous feeling afraid or unsure

recite say something out loud

rehearse practise a show to be ready to perform it to an audience

role actor's part in a film or play

script story for a play, film or television show

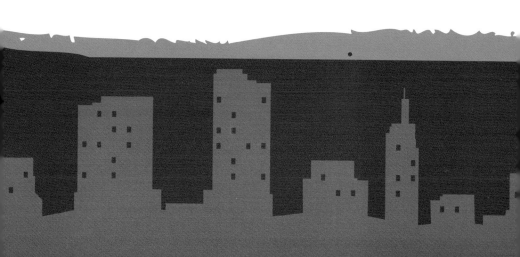

PLAY TIME

If you were the director of a play, what would your play be about? Come up with a title for your play and a list of different roles. Then write a few lines for your actors to memorise. Ask your friends or family to help you act each role. Swap roles with your friends and act each one until you find the role you like best.

LET'S TALK

1. Imagine you are going to be in a play. What role would you want? How would you get ready for your performance?

2. JC was excited about performing at first, but then he felt nervous. Have you ever felt nervous about trying something new? How did you work through it?

3. Amir and Vicky encourage JC to keep going when he forgets his lines. What do you think makes a good friend? Talk about some different things friends do to support each other.

LET'S WRITE

1. What are some other fun activities JC and his friends could try? Write a list of three new ideas. They can be things you've done with your friends or things you want to try!

2. JC, Vicky and Amir had to audition for their roles in the play. What are some other activities you're interested in that might require an audition? Make a list!

3. Being an actor means memorising lots of lines. Write your own short script and try to memorise it. Then perform it in front of your family and friends!

ABOUT THE CREATORS

Dorothy H Price loves writing stories for young readers. Her first picture book, *Nana's Favorite Things*, is proof of that. Dorothy was a 2019 winner of the We Need Diverse Books Mentorship Program in the United States. She hopes all young readers know they can grow up to write stories too.

Shiane Salabie is a Jamaica-born illustrator based in Philadelphia, USA. When she moved to the United States, she discovered her first true love: the library. Shiane later realized that she wanted to bring stories to life and uses her art to do so.